Regards to the Man in the Moon

EZRA JACK KEATS

Aladdin Paperbacks

"What's up, Louie? Why so sad?"
 Barney asked.
"The kids are laughin' at me."
"Laughin' at you! Why?"
"Well—"
"Come on, you c'n tell me.
 I'm your Pop now."

"Well," Louie said, "they call you the junkman."

"Junk?" Barney growled. "They should know better than to call this junk. All a person needs is some imagination! And a little of that stuff can take you right out of this world. Watta' ya' say, Louie? Wanna give it a try?"

Louie and his parents got to work.
"What's goin' on?" the kids asked.
"I'm goin' outta this world,"
   Louie answered.

The kids snickered and nudged each other.
"Is that Voyager III?" they laughed.
"No," he said, "It's IMAGINATION I!"

"Well, don't run out of gas!"

"Regards to the Man in the Moon," they kidded.

"Are you going out there all alone?" Susie asked.

"Can I come with you, Louie? Can I?"

"Well, that depends—got lots of imagination?" he asked.

"Oh, yes," she said. "And—and I'll bring cookies, too!"
"Hmm, okay! Be here early tomorrow."

The next morning they climbed aboard.
"Ready when you are," Susie shouted.

"Okay then," yelled Louie.
"Blast off!"
They held their breath.

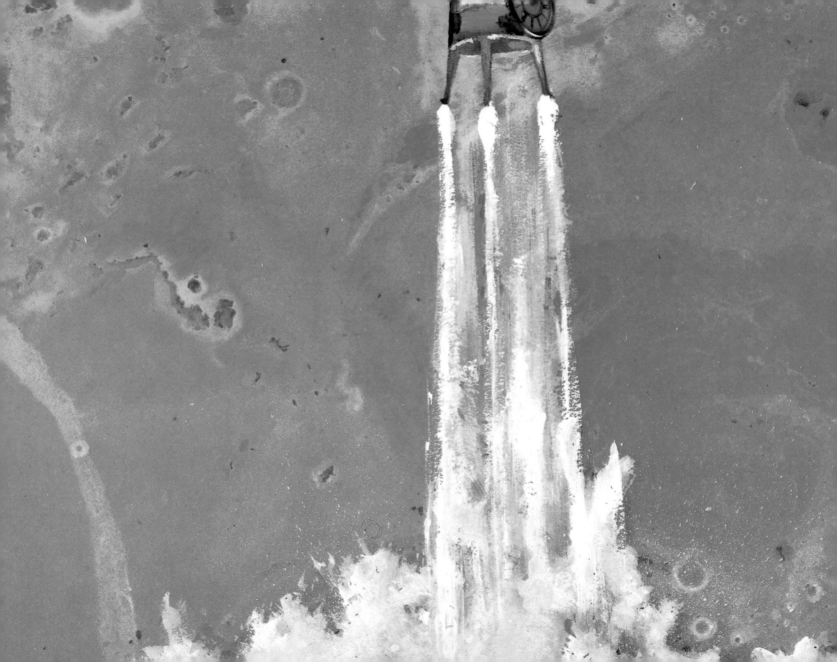

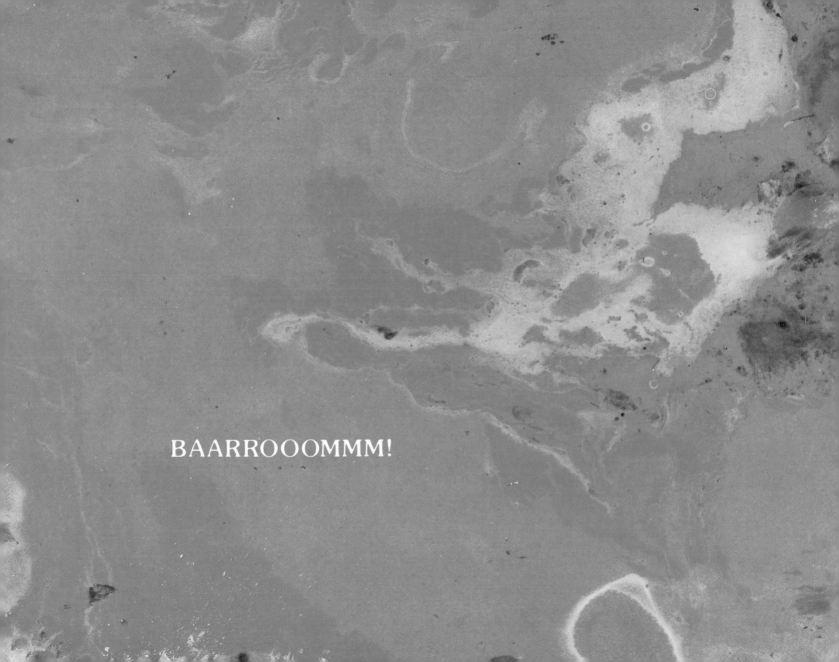

BAARROOOMMM!

Way out in space they opened their eyes.

"We did it!" Susie gasped. They stared down at planet Earth.

"Everybody we know is down there—and we're all alone up here.

I'm scared!"

"Me too!" Louie whispered.

They floated past strange and wondrous things...

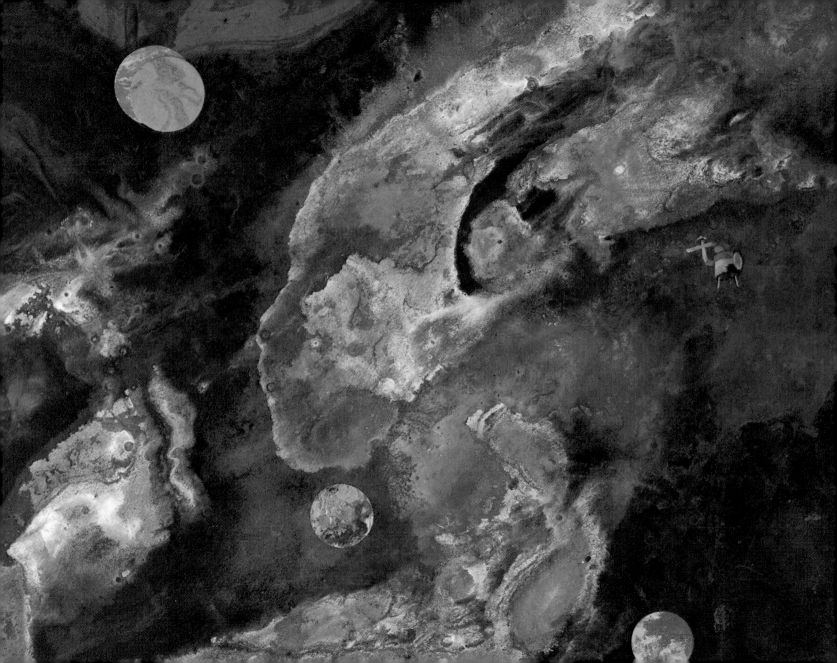

...and on through worlds no one had ever seen before.

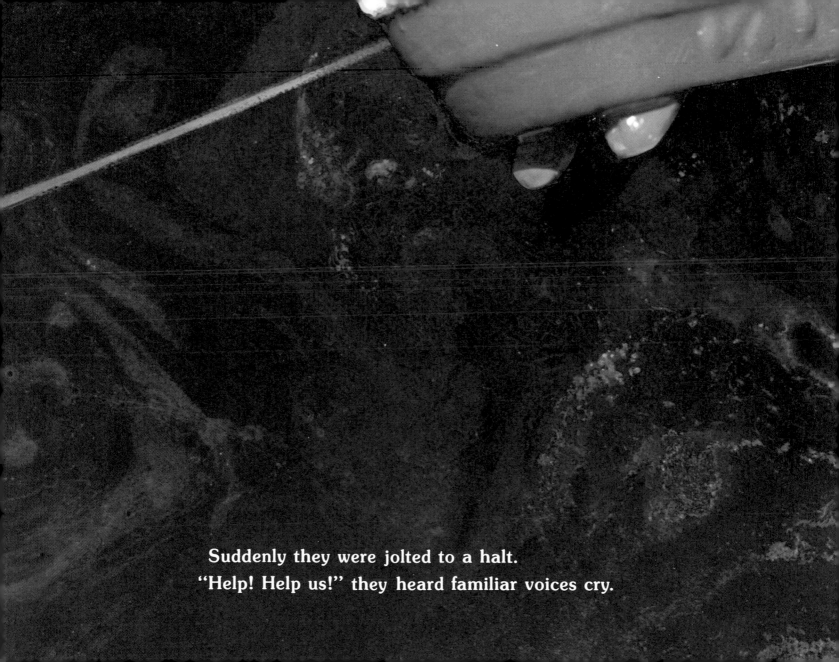

Suddenly they were jolted to a halt.
"Help! Help us!" they heard familiar voices cry.

It was Ziggie and Ruthie.
"We decided to follow you," Ziggie cried.
"But we've used up all our imagination.
We're stuck. We can't move. Don't untie us,
please, or we'll never get home."

"Let go!" Susie yelled.
"Or we'll all be stuck out here forever.
  You can only move on your own imagination!"
"Let go, will ya'," Louie cried. "There's a rock storm
heading this way. We'll be smashed to bits!"

"They're not rocks! Can't you see?
  They're monsters!" Ziggie moaned.
"They're coming to capture us.
  We'll never see home again!"
"Monsters!" Susie said.
"Now you're using your imagination."
  They began to move.
"You're doin' fine now," Susie called, "so let go!
  You'll do better on your own and so will we."
But Ziggie and Ruthie were so scared
  they just hung on.

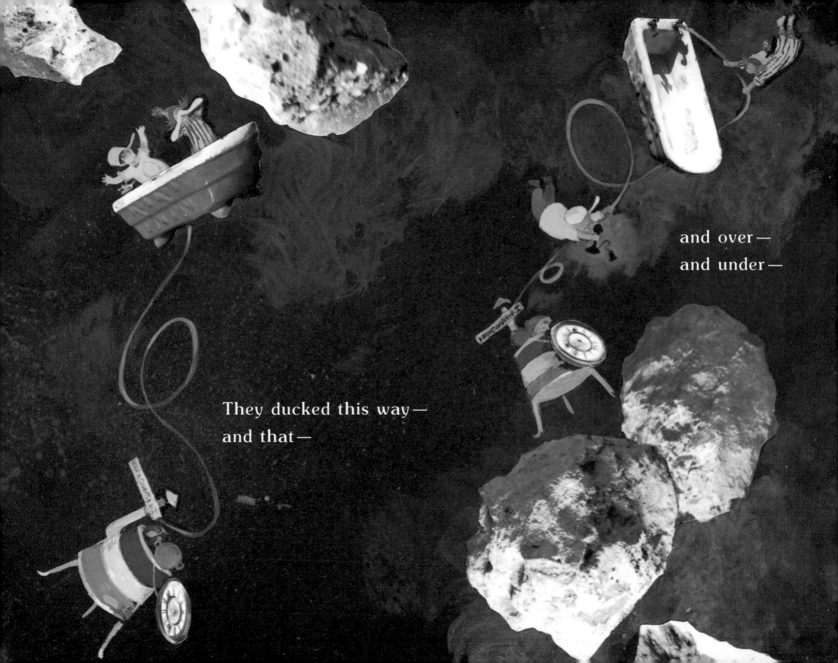

and over—
and under—

They ducked this way—
and that—

and upside down.

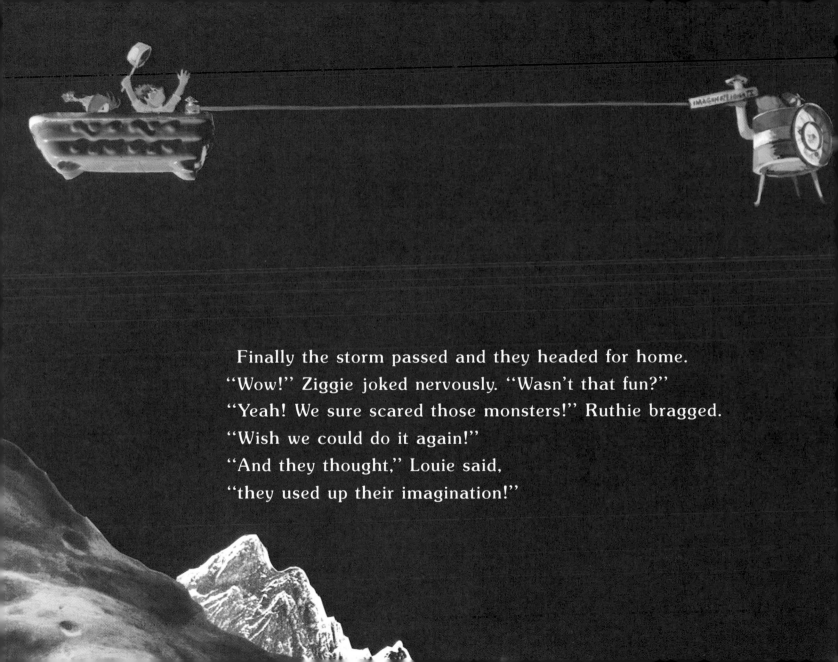

Finally the storm passed and they headed for home.

"Wow!" Ziggie joked nervously. "Wasn't that fun?"

"Yeah! We sure scared those monsters!" Ruthie bragged.

"Wish we could do it again!"

"And they thought," Louie said,

"they used up their imagination!"

They were getting close to home when Ziggie finally dropped the rope.